Almost
Katharine the Great

Swimming
with
the Sharks

by Lisa Mullarkey
illustrated by Phyllis Harris

magic
wagon

visit us at www.abdopublishing.com

Thanks to Collin Geyer for diving in and helping me learn all about swim team.—LM
To Micah and Rachel and all the fun memories in grandma's pool. —PH

Published by Magic Wagon, a division of the ABDO Group, PO Box 398166, Minneapolis, Minnesota 55439. Copyright © 2012 by Abdo Consulting Group, Inc. International copyrights reserved in all countries. All rights reserved. No part of this book may be reproduced in any form without written permission from the publisher.

Calico Chapter Books™ is a trademark and logo of Magic Wagon.

Printed in the United States of America, North Mankato, Minnesota.
092011
012012
This book contains at least 10% recycled materials.

Text by Lisa Mullarkey
Illustrations by Phyllis Harris
Edited by Stephanie Hedlund and Rochelle Baltzer
Interior layout and design by Jaime Martens
Cover design by Jaime Martens

Library of Congress Cataloging-in-Publication Data
Mullarkey, Lisa.
  Swimming with the sharks / by Lisa Mullarkey ; illustrated by Phyllis Harris.
      p. cm. -- (Katharine the Almost Great)
  Summary: When Katharine joins the Stingrays Swim Team she finds herself once again in competition with her schoolmate, Vanessa, who swims for the Sharks.
  ISBN 978-1-61641-832-8
  1. Swimming--Juvenile fiction. 2. Swim clubs--Juvenile fiction. 3. Competition (Psychology)--Juvenile fiction. 4. Schools--Juvenile fiction. 5. Friendship--Juvenile fiction. [1. Swimming--Fiction. 2. Competition (Psychology)--Fiction. 3. Schools--Fiction. 4. Friendship--Fiction.] I. Harris, Phyllis, 1962- ill. II. Title. III. Series: Mullarkey, Lisa. Katharine the Almost Great.
  PZ7.M91148Sw 2012
  [Fic]--dc23
                                                            2011026391

❋ CONTENTS ❋

CHAPTER 1

Butterfly, Shmutterfly

I tap, tap, tapped the poster. "Did you see this, Crockett?"

Crockett shook his head. "I can't see anything."

I squeezed the water out of one of my pigtails. "Of course you can't. Take off your goggles, Frog Face."

Crockett snapped off the goggles. He read the poster.

I jumped up and down. "We're going to be Stingrays!"

Crockett's mouth fell open. "We are?"

I slipped into my flip-flops and asked, "Don't you want to be a Stingray?"

He wiped a drop of water off of his nose. "You can't just *be* a Stingray. You have to try out. It's not easy to make the team." He lowered his goggles and pretended to catch a fly with his tongue. "Ribbit. Ribbit."

"How hard can it be?" I asked. "Easy breezy."

"Easy breezy?" boomed a voice.

We turned around to see a man in an Aqua Boy T-shirt. He held a clipboard in one hand and a stopwatch in the other.

"Easy breezy?" repeated Aqua Boy. "Are you sure?"

My stomach did a flip-flop belly drop. "Maybe not easy breezy . . ."

He smiled. "I hope it is easy breezy for you and your friend. That would mean you're both good swimmers. Good swimmers are fast swimmers. I'm looking for some new Stingrays."

He pointed to his badge. "I'm Coach Geyer." He waved his clipboard in the air. "Want to sign up?"

I wrapped a towel around my waist. "You betcha!" A second later, *Katharine Marie Carmichael* was written neatly on the clipboard. "I've never raced before."

"That's what the clinic's for," said Coach Geyer. "We'll teach you everything you'll need to know. After the first practice, some kids think it's too much work. They don't come back. Others try out but don't make the team."

My heart thumpity thumped.

Coach wrinkled his nose. "They're usually the kids who goof off or are lazy." He leaned forward. "You're not lazy, are you?"

Didn't he see the hearts I used to dot the *i* in my name? A lazy person does not draw hearts!

I shook my head from side to side. Then I remembered some crazy-o lazy-o stuff. But I zipped my lips! He didn't need to know about the weeklong Penelope Parks movie marathon I watched over the holidays. Or the clean clothes I stashed under my bed. Stashing is way easier than hanging.

But I didn't want to lie. My voice cracked. "I'm not a lazy swimmer. And I won't goof off."

"Are you positive?" asked Coach Geyer.

I flashed my biggest smile. "Positively positive!"

He scribbled something down on the clipboard. "What grade are you in?"

"Third," I answered.

More scribbling.

Then he looked Crockett up and down. "Are you trying out? You're tall. You look like a swimmer."

I stood as straight as a diving board. I was at least an inch taller. Maybe two!

"I can't," said Crockett. "I have Junior Rangers meetings next week."

Coach Geyer patted Crockett's back. "Well, you're in luck, kid. Because the clinic and tryouts are *this* week. That poster was hung up last week."

Crockett's face brightened. "Really?"

"So that's a yes?" asked Coach Geyer.

Crockett nodded. "Ribbit."

Coach Geyer pulled papers off of the clipboard. "Have your parents read and sign these. I'll see you both tomorrow night at seven o'clock."

I raised my arms and pretended to swim away. "Thanks, Coach."

"That's freestyle," he said. "Don't forget about butterfly, backstroke, and breaststroke."

"Backstroke?" I gulped. "Breaststroke?" I gasped. "I'm not good at those. I can't do the butterfly stroke at all."

"Don't worry," he said. "That's what practices are for. Fly is the hardest stroke. It takes a long time to nail it." He pointed to a girl swimming in lane three. "Look at her butterfly." He stepped closer to the pool. "She shoots through the water like a torpedo!"

"Must be a high school kid," said Crockett.

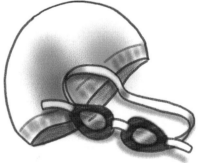

When the swimmer got to the end of the lane, she

tore off her goggles. She pumped her fist in the air.

Everyone clapped.

Everyone but me.

Because it wasn't a highschooler. It was a third grader. And not just any third grader.

It was Miss Priss-A-Poo.

Vanessa Garfinkle!

Coach Geyer's eyes lit up. He rushed over to her as he waved his clipboard.

Butterfly, shmutterfly.

I wanted to flutter away.

❀ CHAPTER 2 ❀

The Creature from the Blue Pool

"The swim team?" asked Dad at dinner. He glanced at Mom and Aunt Chrissy. "I had no idea you kids wanted to compete."

"Me either," said Aunt Chrissy. She scooped potatoes onto her plate. "I met Coach Geyer when I picked them up." She pointed at some papers with the potato spoon. "He gave us these to look over."

Mom smooshed Jack's carrots. "How often will you have practice?"

Aunt Chrissy scanned the sheet. "Three nights a week and once over the weekend."

Mom frowned. "That's an awful lot." She handed Jack his sippy cup. "What about homework, Katharine? And don't forget about getting tutored by Mrs. Curtin."

This is what I wanted to say:

"Who needs homework and tutoring when you're going to be an Olympic swimmer?"

But this is what I really said:

"I doubt I'll make the team." I thought about Vanessa. "I can't do the butterfly stroke."

"A lot of kids can't do it," said Crockett. "You heard what the coach said."

"Vanessa can do it," I mumbled. "She's fast, too." I pushed my plate away.

Mom used her thundery voice. "If you're giving up before you even begin then . . ."

Crockett kicked me under the table.

I cleared my throat. "I'm not giving up, Mom. Promise!"

"We still have to make the team," Crockett reminded me. "And they haven't signed our papers yet."

"I vote yes," said Aunt Chrissy. She signed Crockett's permission slip. "It's great exercise."

Dad agreed. "It is great exercise. But . . ."

"But what?" I asked.

He threw his hands up in the air. "You can be lazy when it comes to exercise. You e-mailed your mom to ask what we were having for dinner."

I ran my fingers across the table. "I was just practicing my keyboarding. I want to get an A."

"But your mother was only in the next room!"

I slid down in my seat. Coach Geyer better not find out about that!

Dad kept talking. "Remember the time you had Crockett pull you to school in a wagon because you were too tired to walk two blocks?"

I had to think fast. "Did you know that elephants can swim twenty miles a day? They use their trunks as snorkels." My useless facts calendar was per-fect-o for times like this!

No one seemed to care.

"Please?" I begged. "I'll never be lazy again. Promise. I'll start homework the second I get home from school."

Jack clapped. "Yeth." Then he smash, smash, smashed his carrots on his head.

Mom winced. "Well, if it's okay with Jack, I guess it's okay with us."

Crockett and I cheered. I gave Jack a big kiss-a-roo. I was so excited that I forgot all about the butterfly stroke.

Until Vanessa rang our doorbell after dinner.

She held out a small bottle. "Use this on your goggles. It'll keep the fog away."

"Thanks, Vanessa," said Crockett. "Are you trying out for the Stingrays? You're a fast swimmer."

She shook her head. "I'm already on the Sharks at Manno's Pool Club. Our pool's filter broke. We had to practice at the Y."

"So you don't usually swim at the Y?" I asked.

"Never," said Vanessa. "We have our own pool at Manno's."

I suddenly felt a little better about this whole butterfly thing. "So we won't be on the same team?"

"*If* we make the team," said Crockett.

"Nope," she said. "That would have been fun, though."

I was feeling a lot better now! "Yep. It would have been. I wanted to race against you. My butterfly stroke is my best stroke, too. But now that you're on the Sharks, I guess I'll never get to show you." I let out one of those super-duper dramatic Penelope Parks sighs.

But I was relieved. Relieved with a capital *R*.

Crockett looked at me like I was the Creature from the Blue Pool.

Vanessa sucked in her breath. "You swim fly?"

I turned to Crockett. "That's the nickname we butterfliers give it. Right, Vanessa?"

Vanessa nodded. "Do you know how swim team works? The Sharks and the Stingrays do compete against each other."

I felt like someone dunked me underwater. "We do?"

"Isn't that great?" said Vanessa. "We'll get to swim the 50 fly together."

"Fifty fly?" I stammered. I didn't even know what that meant.

Vanessa hesitated. "Unless you swim the 100 fly. I can't do the 100 yet. I get too tired."

"Yep. Katharine does the 100 fly. Right, Katharine?" Crockett had a smirk on his face. It was a serves-you-right-for-lying kind of smirk.

"Gotta go," said Vanessa. She hopped down the steps, turned around, and waved. "I'll see you tomorrow night."

"Tomorrow night?" I whispered. "Do you mean Monday at school?"

"Our filter won't be fixed until next week," said Vanessa. "So we'll be swimming together all week!"

Crockett closed the door and laughed. "Once Vanessa finds out you lied, you'll be swimming with the sharks."

"Worse," I said. "I'll be shark bait."

❀ CHAPTER 3 ❀

Ker-plop!

We hopped out of the car at 6:58 the next night.

"Good luck," said Aunt Chrissy. "Have fun."

I thought about Vanessa. How much fun could I have when I was about to be called a Cheatie Girl?

Before we opened the door to the pool, I stopped Crockett. "What if I sink to the bottom?"

"You won't sink."

I peeked through the door. Johnny and Tamara were in the pool. They made the team last year. "What if I forget to move my arms? Or forget to kick my legs?"

He pushed the door open. "Then you will sink." He laughed.

It was not a chuckle moment.

Coach Geyer waved us over. "Where's your cap, Katharine? It keeps your hair out of your face when you swim."

I pulled the cap out of my bag.

He grabbed it and dunked it in the pool. "It's easier to put on when it's wet."

With a quick wiggle, wiggle, wiggle, it was on.

"If you make the team, Crockett, you'll need one for meets," said Coach Geyer. "Now jump in and warm up."

Crockett did a cannonball into the pool. Then he started to swim the backstroke.

Show-off.

I stuck my toe in the deep end. "It's freezing! Isn't the heater working?"

Coach Geyer laughed. "I lower the temperature when we practice or have meets. Cold water makes you swim faster."

I waited until he walked away before jumping into the pool.

"It's so cold in here," I yelled to Crockett. My teeth chattered.

"Don't let the coach think you're lazy, Katharine," said Johnny. "Swim."

"He doesn't like lazy swimmers," said Tamara as she floated by.

I used my feet to push off the wall and swam the whole lap underwater.

When I came to the surface, Coach Geyer was waiting.

"Now that you're warmed up, let's see what you can do. Everyone out of the pool."

Oodles and oodles of dripping kids huddled around him.

"I'm timing everyone swimming the 25 and 50 freestyle. The 25 is when you swim from one side to the other. It's 25 yards."

"I get it," said Crockett. "The 50 is when you go back and forth."

"Yep," said Tamara.

"It's up to you whether you want to do a grab or track start," said Coach Geyer.

"A grab what?" I asked. "A truck start?"

He tucked his clipboard under his arm. "Unless you're swimming backstroke, you get into the water by diving off the starting block." He stepped onto it. "This is a grab start." He squatted and curled his toes and fingers over the edge of the block. "Katharine, come up and show me a grab start."

"Me? I don't think . . ."

Coach Geyer folded his arms and gave me his grumpy eyes.

I slowly stepped onto the block and leaned over. Before I could grab the edge, I tumbled into the water.

Splash!

Everyone laughed.

Except Coach Geyer. "That can happen to anyone." He bent down and held out his hand. I grabbed it and climbed back onto the deck.

He pointed to the block. "If at first you don't succeed, try, try again."

My knees wobbled as I stepped back onto the block. This time, I grabbed it with my hands, curled my toes around the edge, and held on tight.

"Good form, Katharine. Now, to get into the water, lean forward and push off as hard as you can with your feet. Extend your arms like this."

He looked more like Super Boy than Aqua Boy.

"Notice how my arms squish up against my ears. Then *swoosh*! Glide through the water." He pointed to the pool. "Try it."

I pushed off with my feet but I didn't swoosh. Or swish. Or glide anywhere. I did a great big belly flop.

Ker-plop!

Everyone laughed.

Even Coach Geyer. "Keep trying."

Then he had Johnny show us a track start. "It looks like you're getting ready to run a race."

As I watched a few more kids practice their starts, the Sharks walked in. Vanessa waved before jumping into the water.

I watched her swim the butterfly. She was quicky quick.

"Katharine, you're up. Lane three," said Coach Geyer.

I jumped up on the block and decided to use a track start. Out of the corner of my eye, I saw Vanessa watching. I lowered my goggles.

"Swimmers, ready? Go!" shouted Coach Geyer.

I jumped into the pool and started swimming. When I finished the lap, I heard Crockett cheering me on. I stood up, turned around, and swam back the other way.

"That was 47.3 seconds," said Coach Geyer as he moved on to the next swimmer.

The Sharks circled around me as I got out of the pool.

"DQ," said the tallest Shark.

"DQ," said the smallest Shark.

Vanessa patted me on the back. "Don't worry about it."

Me? Worry? About what? Didn't DQ mean ice cream? After all, a super-duper job deserves ice cream, doesn't it? "What's a DQ?"

"You broke a rule," said Vanessa. "You can't stand or walk in the pool while you're racing. DQ means you're disqualified."

No ice cream for me. Coach Geyer was right. Making the swim team wasn't going to be easy breezy.

Looking around, I saw the Sharks practicing a relay race. Crockett and Tamara were diving into the pool without a belly flop in sight. Coach Geyer was giving Johnny a high five.

Disqualified?

A tear dripped.

A tear dropped.

I jumped back into the pool and swam as fast as I could.

I wanted to swim all the way to China.

Meanie Girl

The next day at school, Vanessa had on a #1 Swimmer shirt.

"Nice shirt," said Crockett. He gave her a thumbs-up.

My thumbs didn't move.

Vanessa fluff-a-puffed her hair. "Thanks! Sorry I didn't get to talk to you last night. Our coach thought we were goofing off. We had to swim extra laps."

Rebecca sniffed the air. "What smells like chlorine?" She sneezed.

"My hair," said Vanessa. "I couldn't find my cap last night. The chlorine smell is stuck in my hair." She called Tamara over. "Did you know Katharine swims the 100 fly?"

"Really?" said Tamara.

I sorta kinda nodded.

"You'll definitely make the team," said Tamara. "No one in our age group can do that. That's amazing."

I didn't feel amazing. I felt like a Cheatie Girl.

"Make what team?" asked Mrs. Bingsley as she wrote the date on the board.

"The Stingrays swim team," said Crockett.

"I'm on the Sharks," said Vanessa. "Tamara and Johnny are on the Stingrays. The same team Crockett and Katharine are trying out for." She grabbed my hand. "Katharine and I both swim fly."

"I can see it now," said Mrs. Bingsley. "Future gold medal winners! Maybe I'll be able to come to one of your meets."

Crockett pretended to pull his hair out. "We haven't made the team yet."

"Think positive," said Mrs. Bingsley.

"And cross your fingers," said Vanessa. "I'll be rooting for you tonight."

The bell rang. Everyone skedaddled to our seats. After the pledge, Mrs. Bingsley called us over to the carpet. "Speaking of stingrays and sharks, we're about to start our ocean unit. Today, everyone will pick a topic out of this hat. You'll read a book about your animal. Then, you'll write five interesting facts about it."

"I hope I get a shark," said Crockett.

"Me too," said Johnny.

"Me three," said Matthew.

I clenched my fists. Sharks sure were pop, pop, popular.

"This is just a warm-up for our first research project," said Mrs. Bingsley. "We'll share our facts. Once you hear everyone's, you'll each choose the animal you want to write about."

Crockett picked first. "Flashlight fish."

Vanessa scooped up a piece of paper. "Bottle-nosed dolphin."

"Orca whale," said Tamara.

I picked last. I reached in and pulled out a crumply paper. "Hammerhead shark."

Vanessa giggled.

Johnny giggled.

Tamara giggled.

I did not giggle.

Crockett patted me on the back. "I wonder if your hammerhead does the butterfly stroke."

I stuck my tongue out at him and grabbed a shark book.

It was a thick book. I scanned the table of contents. "Five Cool Facts About Sharks" was on page 96.

I flipped to the page and read:

1. Hammerhead sharks use their uniquely shaped heads to attack stingrays. They pin the winged fish against the ocean floor.

   Attack stingrays? How mean!

2. Hammerhead sharks can detect the electrical fields created by animals. This helps them find their favorite dinner: stingrays! Stingrays usually bury themselves under the sand. But

they can't hide from the powerful hammerhead shark!

Sharks eat stingrays? Disgust-o! I did not like that! Not one itty-bitty bit.

I was doomed!

I glared at Vanessa. I decided I did not like sharks. Not great white sharks. Not hammerhead sharks. Not Sharks who yell DQ. And especially not Sharks who swim the butterfly stroke.

I slammed the book shut and wrote my own facts.

"Put your books down, kids," said Mrs. Bingsley thirty minutes later. "You've had plenty of time to read and write facts." She walked over to the carpet. "Let's share them."

My stomach did a flip-flop belly drop. If Mrs. Bingsley saw my fake facts, I'd be in mega mucho trouble. Trouble with a capital *T*.

Katharine's Shark Facts

1. Sharks like to show off and brag they are #1.

2. Penelope Parks hates sharks. Her most favorite animals are stingrays.

3. Sharks think Berrylicious Lip Gloss is the best in the world. But Stingrays know that Luscious Lemon Lip Gloss is better. (And Penelope's favorite.)

4. Sharks smell like chlorine and make their friends sneeze.

5. Sharks are lazy. They can only swim a 50 fly. Coach Geyer would not want a lazy shark on his team.

I glanced at the clock. Library was in six minutes. Maybe we'd run out of time. I crossed my fingers. Lily was first. Then we listened to Crockett, Rebecca, Tamara, Diego, and Matthew.

Three minutes left.

Caroline and Elizabeth shared their facts.

Two minutes.

Julia talked about starfish.

One minute.

Mrs. Bingsley stood. "That's all we have time for today."

I let out a sigh of relief.

The bell rang.

Saved by the bell!

Or so I thought.

I felt someone breathing on my neck.

When I turned around, I saw scary shark teeth.

"That's mean, Katharine," said Vanessa. "Really, *really* mean." She slowly walked to the door.

My face burned. It was mean. Really, really, really mean.

I wasn't just a Cheatie Girl. I was a Meanie Girl.

I wanted to bury myself under a pile of sand.

CHAPTER 5

The Unsinkable Garfinkle

Vanessa wouldn't talk to me for the rest of the day.

She picked Rebecca for partner reading. And Rebecca didn't even have the new Penelope Parks biography. I did!

When I tried to give her a cookie at lunch, she pushed my hand away.

She was mad.

"Would you like it if she wrote nasty things about stingrays?" asked Crockett after lunch.

He was right.

Again.

"If Mrs. Bingsley finds out, you'll have to go see Ammer the Hammer," said Crockett. "She doesn't like bullies."

Ammer the Hammer was Mrs. Ammer, our principal. I did not want to have another chitchat with her.

"Bullies? I didn't mean to bully Vanessa. I was just . . . just . . . "

"Jealous?" said Crockett.

I nodded. "A little."

He put his hands on his hips and cocked his head. "A lot."

Instead of going to recess, I made Vanessa a snazzly dazzly card. I drew a picture of her and Sparky with Mrs. Bingsley and her new cat. On the inside, I wrote:

Five Facts About the Amazing Vanessa Garfinkle

1. She is the best artist in our class. Her art should be in a museum. She can draw the Mona Lisa way better than that Da Vinci boy.

2. Coach Geyer said that she is the best "10 and under" fly swimmer in the state of New Jersey. I bet it's the whole world. She's the Unsinkable Garfinkle!

3. When she swims, she looks like a beautiful mermaid. She's even prettier than Penelope Parks!

4. Her teeth are shiny and bright. She smells like Berrylicious Lip Gloss. Not stinky chlorine.

5. She is kind and caring to everyone and everything. She adopted her dog from a shelter. When Frankie wanted to stomp on ants, she stopped him. She said, "Ants have feelings, too."

I'm sorry I hurt your feelings. From the one and only, Katharine the Almost Great

I thought about what Crockett said. Maybe if I apologized, my parents would call me Katharine the Great.

I slipped the card into her desk. But if she read it, she never let me know.

"Can you blame her?" asked Mom after school. "That wasn't very nice of you."

Dad sighed. "But we're glad you told us. We know you're sorry."

"Really, really sorry," I said. "For lying, too."

"Katharine!" shrieked Mom. "Who did you lie to?"

"She told Vanessa she could swim the butterfly stroke," said Crockett.

Aunt Chrissy rolled her eyes. "Why?"

I shrugged. "When I swim tonight, she'll know. She'll hate me even more."

"Vanessa doesn't hate you," said Crockett. "Just apologize."

"I did. In the card." I picked at my food. "I guess you're going to make me quit, aren't you, Mom?"

This is what I thought she'd say:

"Yep. You acted like a bully. Bullies don't deserve to be on any team."

But this is what she really said:

"Nope. We all make mistakes. You're not a quitter."

"Quitters never win," said Dad, "and winners never quit. Face your fears, Katharine. Learn the butterfly stroke. Practice. And apologize."

"She'll talk to you at practice tonight," said Crockett. "You'll see."

But I was so busy, I didn't even see Vanessa until the end of practice.

We started off by swimming freestyle. This time, I made sure not to walk in the pool or stand when I had to turn around. No more DQs for me!

"Let's see your breaststroke," said Coach Geyer.

Then I had to swim the backstroke.

Swimming the backstroke was hard. I kept hitting the ropes. I couldn't swim in a straight line. I crossed the lane and swam right into Tamara.

Smack!

"Ouch," said Tamara. "You poked me in the eye."

"Sorry! I can't see where I'm going."

She pointed to the ceiling. "Use the flags up there. They're in a straight line. Follow them and you'll stay in your lane."

That was a fab-u-lo-so trick!

By the time I finally made it to the other side, my arms felt like wiggly, squiggly spaghetti. I climbed out of the pool.

"Where are you going?" asked Coach Geyer. "You need to swim the other 25."

"I have to swim all the way back there? On my back?"

He nodded. "You can do it."

I veered to the left. Then the right. Finally, I remembered the flags! But when I looked up, I felt dizzy.

"Keep going," said Coach Geyer. "Don't quit on me."

I remembered what Dad said. Quitters never win and winners never quit. I wanted to win. I kicked harder. I moved my arms faster. Finally, I hit the wall.

"That was terrible," I said. "It took me forever."

"Not forever. Just over two minutes," Coach Geyer said. "You're a beginner. Right now, I'm more interested in seeing your attitude than your time."

And just like that, Coach made me feel like a winner!

When I went to get a drink, I saw Vanessa sitting on the bleachers. I walked over to her.

"Sorry for today, Vanessa. And for being a Cheatie Girl. I lied. I can't swim fly. You're so good, you're the Unsinkable Garfinkle!"

Vanessa burst into tears.

My throat felt lumpy. Bumpy. "I really, really, really am sorry! I didn't mean to make you cry. Honest."

Vanessa blew her nose. "I've got big problems."

I patted her on the back. "But you're the Unsinkable Garfinkle!"

"I'm not a Shark anymore."

Oops.

The Unsinkable Garfinkle just sank.

Shark Bite

"Then what happened?" asked Crockett on the car ride home. "Did she really burst into tears like that?"

I nodded. I told Crockett and Dad, "She walked over to her mom. Then they left. I have no idea why her coach kicked her off of the team."

Dad pulled into our driveway. "Don't jump to conclusions. Maybe she quit," he said.

"She didn't quit," I said. "I'm positive."

Dad raised his eyebrow.

"Positively positive," I said.

"We'll find out in school tomorrow," said Crockett.

But we didn't find out in school. Vanessa was absent.

"Did the rest of the Sharks leave at the same time as Vanessa yesterday?" asked Tamara at lunch.

Johnny shook his head. "They were still swimming when I left," he said.

"Are you sure she wasn't mad at you for your shark facts?" asked Tamara. She narrowed her eyes. "That was mean, Katharine."

My lip quivered. How did she know about them? "I apologized. Besides, she said she had bigger problems." I thought about my card. "Did she tell you I made new amazing facts about her?"

Tamara shook her head.

Rats.

"Are you guys nervous?" asked Johnny. "Coach Geyer is posting the swim team names tonight."

I stopped chewing. "*Tonight?* Are you sure?" My stomach felt all splishy splashy inside.

"Yep. Then we get ready for our meet on Saturday. He needs time to decide who's swimming what race."

Forget Vanessa. Now *I* had bigger things to worry about. And I worried all the way to practice that night.

Aunt Chrissy dropped us off at 6:50. "Good luck, kids! Remember, if you don't make it, you can try out again next year. I'm proud of both of you no matter what happens."

"If I don't make it," I said, "I'm swimming to China."

As soon as we walked onto the deck, we saw everyone crowded around Coach Geyer.

He waved us over and started to count each swimmer. "Great! Everyone's here."

"Not everyone," I said. "You know that kid who liked to sit on the starting block? He's not here."

"Olivia what's-her-name isn't here either," said Tamara. "She's the one who came late to practice. Twice. She wouldn't wear her cap either."

"Exactly," said Coach Geyer. "They aren't coming. Ten other kids aren't coming either. I called their parents today to break the news to them. They didn't make the team."

Pish posh, I thought. *Too bad for them.*

"But if you're here tonight," said Coach Geyer, *"congratulations!* You're now officially a member of the Stingrays Swim Team."

Tamara and I did a victory dance!

Crockett and Johnny chest bumped and high-fived each other.

"You're all on the team for two reasons," said Coach Geyer. "You have talent and you're hard workers. Remember my number one rule. We're here to have fun." He pointed to the pool. "Now everyone give me your best cannonball. Last one in is a slimy eel."

I rush-a-rooed into the pool but guess who was the slimy eel. Me!

The celebration didn't last long. A minute later, Coach Geyer pulled me aside. "You have to learn how to do a flip turn."

My heart raced. I wrinkled my nose. "Do I have to?"

"You'll get a DQ if your feet touch the floor of the pool. You're a great freestyle swimmer. You'll be even faster once you use a flip turn."

"My friend Vanessa never does a flip turn when she swims fly."

"The breaststroke and butterfly rules are different. You'll need to do an open turn for them. No flips allowed. You'll touch the wall with both hands. Then you'll push off the wall. If you don't do a two-hand touch, they'll call a DQ." He patted my back. "But since you're swimming freestyle, you'll have to learn to flip."

"I don't like water up my nose. It burns. It's disgust-o. Disgust-o with a capital *D*."

He dug something out

of his pocket. "Here's a nose clip. It keeps the water out."

After twenty minutes of practicing somersaults underwater, I could almost do a flip turn.

"You're a quick learner," said Coach Geyer. "That's one of the reasons you made the team."

I was about to practice my butterfly stroke when I saw the Sharks walk in. They were all there except for Vanessa.

I jumped out of the pool and walked up to the coach. "Coach Gabby? I'm Katharine. I'm on the Stingrays."

Coach Gabby held out her hand and said, "Congratulations. I've been watching you swim."

"Thanks!" I shook her hand. Then I asked, "Why did you kick Vanessa off of your team? She's a hard worker. And she's not the kind of kid to goof around. Or be lazy. And she's not a bully."

Coach Gabby's eyes grew wide. "Who said I kicked her off the team?"

"Vanessa said she wasn't a Shark anymore. She's not a quitter. So, I thought . . . "

"Well, you thought wrong, Katharine. And I can't share private information with you. You understand, don't you?" Then she put her hands on her hips and squinted her eyes. "Are you the same Katharine who wrote those nasty shark facts?"

Ouch.

How did she know?

"Did you know that the first goggles were made from polished tortoise shells?" I asked.

She didn't seem to care. "Be nice to Vanessa. No bullies allowed in swimming."

Bullies?

I had been bitten by a shark.

Again.

CHAPTER 7

S.A.S.

When Vanessa walked into school, she looked grump, grump, grumpy. She unpacked without saying a word. When Mrs. Bingsley asked how she felt, she shrugged.

"Are you okay?" I asked. "What happened?"

Her lips were zipped.

Again.

I could see my card inside her desk.

"We have lots of work today, kids," said Mrs. Bingsley. "Take out your math books and start page 226."

But I didn't work on page 226. I ripped off a small piece of paper and wrote:

Did you read the card? I'm sorry. Sorrier-than-I've-ever-been-before sorry. Honest.

I tossed the note to her. It landed in her lap.

Vanessa opened the note. She wrote something back and threw it. It hit me in the eye.

What card?

I turned the paper over and wrote:

The card I put in your desk.

Then I drew a heart on it and flicked it to her.

She read it and then peeked inside her desk.

Mrs. Bingsley stopped writing on the board. "Do you need something, Vanessa?"

Vanessa shook her head back and forth.

Mrs. Bingsley bit her lip. She glanced at me and then back at Vanessa. "If anyone needs help, ask."

I started to work on the problems. But Vanessa didn't. She looked for the card.

Out came a shark eraser, a Penelope Parks pencil case, and a tube of Luscious Lemon Lip Gloss.

My lost lip gloss!

She smirked. Then she opened the tube. With a swoosh and a whoosh, she slathered it all over her mouth. After she licked her lips, she stuck her tongue out at me!

Then she saw the card. She pulled it out of her desk and read it.

She smiled. A great, big, goof-a-roo kind of smile.

I smiled back.

"Sorry," I mouthed.

"That's okay," she whispered.

But the smiling didn't last long.

I tossed her another note.

I'm sorry the coach kicked you off of your team.

Vanessa's smile slip slided away. Her cheeks turned red. Then purple. She huff-a-puffed her chest and yelled, "I did not get kicked off the Sharks!"

Mrs. Bingsley dropped her chalk.

Crockett threw his pencil up in the air.

"Oops," I whispered. I wanted to hide my head in the sand.

Mrs. Bingsley pursed her lips. "May I see you in the hallway, Vanessa?"

Vanessa shuffled to the door.

Two minutes later, Mrs. Bingsley poked her nose inside. "Katharine, may I see you?"

Vanessa stood in the hallway. Her arms were folded. She growled, "I did not get kicked off the team."

"Take a deep breath, Vanessa," said Mrs. Bingsley. "Count to ten."

Vanessa sucked in the biggest breath ever. About a minute later, she exhaled. She could hold her breath forever!

"Manno's swim team is moving. Our pool has so many problems that it can't be used anymore. Coach Gabby said it isn't safe. She found another pool to use."

"That's good," I said.

"But it's 35 minutes away. A lot of the kids live near it. But my parents said it's too far away."

"Oh, that's bad," I said.

"So I had to quit."

"But you're not a quitter," I said. I thought about my dad. "Quitters never win and winners never quit."

Mrs. Bingsley put her arm around Vanessa's shoulder. "I wouldn't call this quitting. Sometimes we can't continue with something no matter how much we want to."

"But she's a great swimmer," I said. "Did you know that she's the best fly swimmer in our age group in New Jersey? She's the Unsinkable Garfinkle!"

"Wow!" said Mrs. Bingsley. "Impressive. I'm sure you'll find another team."

That's when I had a lightbulb moment.

"Join the Stingrays," I said. "Coach Geyer will let you."

She shook her head. "I didn't try out for his team. Coach Gabby says that if a kid doesn't take the time to try out, then they can't be on the team."

"You didn't try out because you were already on a team," I said. "Coach Geyer knows that. He's a smart cookie. He watched you swim. He knows how good you are."

"Think so?" asked Vanessa.

I nodded.

"Do you think he'll ask me to be on the team?" said Vanessa.

Mrs. Bingsley hugged her. "You know what they say, 'Don't wait for your ship to come in. Swim out to it.'"

"Huh?" I said.

"Double huh?" said Vanessa.

Mrs. Bingsley laughed. "Don't wait for him to ask you. You need to ask him."

I nodded. "We need to send him an S.A.S."

Vanessa looked confused. "Do you mean an S.O.S?"

"Nope. An S.A.S. . . . Save a Shark."

Stingrays Rule the Pool

"That's a great idea," said Tamara at lunch. "I've always wanted you to be a Stingray. Now you will be." She high-fived Vanessa.

"Coach Geyer will definitely want you on our team," said Johnny. "No one swims fly like you."

Crockett poked Vanessa in her arm. "Zzzzzap!"

Vanessa rubbed it. "Zzzzzap?"

"That's the official Stingray welcome," said Crockett. "If we sting each other, we won't get stung by anyone else. We'll win every meet."

We took turns zapping each other. I gave Vanessa two zaps.

"Do you want us to drive you tonight?" asked Crockett. "We can walk in together."

"That would be great," said Vanessa. She crossed her fingers. "I hope Coach Geyer lets me join."

I crossed my fingers, too. And my toes, legs, and arms. "I think you should wear all of your ribbons and medals. That way, he'll be able to see how good you really are."

"All of them?" asked Vanessa.

"Yep! All of them," I said. "I heard you have zillions."

"Bring your scrapbook," said Tamara. "You have all the articles from the newspaper, don't you?"

Vanessa nodded.

"Don't forget to bring your autographed Michael Phelps poster," said Johnny. "Coach Geyer will be very impressed. He thinks Michael Phelps is the best swimmer in the world."

"I'll bring it," she said.

"Wear your purple goggles and your sparkly cap," I added. "Just in case."

"Just in case what?" asked Johnny.

Tamara shrugged. Crockett shrugged. I shrugged, too.

Then we all laughed. It was a chuckle moment. I heart chuckle moments!

When we picked Vanessa up, we hardly recognized her. She already had on her sparkly swim cap with #1 Swimmer stitched on the front. "I brought my lucky goggles," she said as she put them on.

"Now you look like the Creature from the Blue Pool," I said.

Then Vanessa unzipped her jacket. Oodles and oodles of medals hung around her neck.

"You won all of those?" I asked. I stopped counting when I got to twenty-six. "There's too many to count!"

"Too many?" asked Vanessa. She waved her Michael Phelps poster in the air. "Maybe I should take some off?"

"Leave them on," I said. "They look great." Then I handed her the S.A.S. card I made.

"Thanks, Katharine! I love how you drew the shark."

It felt so much better writing nice things instead of bully things. It made me feel all comfy cozy inside.

Aunt Chrissy spoke up. "Be yourself, Vanessa. You're a great swimmer and a hard worker. You have a lot to be proud of. Coach Geyer would be proud to have you on the team."

When we got out of the car, Aunt Chrissy yelled, "Good luck!"

But Vanessa didn't need any luck.

Coach Geyer grinned when he saw her. "I was talking to Coach Gabby yesterday. We were hoping you'd show up today. I'd love to have you join the Stingrays."

"Just like that?" asked Vanessa.

"Just like that," said Coach Geyer. "Unless you want to take tests, show me your best belly flop, and hold your breath underwater for two minutes?"

"No thanks," said Vanessa.

"Then welcome to the Stingrays," said Coach.

"Three cheers for Vanessa!" yelled Tamara.

Everyone cheered. I cheered the loudest.

"Time to get to work," said Coach Geyer. "Let's see what you can do."

After Vanessa took off her medals, she dove into the water. She started to swim fly.

Coach Geyer blew his whistle. He held his hand up. "Stop." He called her over. "I know you can swim fly. But I need you to swim other strokes, too."

Vanessa pushed her goggles up on her forehead. "Other strokes?"

He nodded. "A girl cannot live by butterfly alone."

Vanessa sighed and pulled herself out of the pool. "Backstroke?" she gulped. "Breaststroke?" She gasped. "I'm not good at those. I can't do the freestyle at all."

I couldn't believe my ears. I wiggled and jiggled them with my finger.

Coach Geyer said, "Don't worry. That's what practices are for."

He pointed to me. "Jump into lane three, Katharine. Show Vanessa your freestyle. After you swim a few laps, I want you to work together. Vanessa will help you with butterfly and you'll help her with freestyle." He scribbled on his clipboard. "Do you two work well together?"

Tamara threw her hands up in the air. "I'm not saying a word."

Johnny laughed. "Me either."

"Leave me out of it," said Crockett.

Coach Geyer looked at me and Vanessa. "Well, do you?"

Vanessa gave me a humongous, ginormus hug-a-rooni. "You betcha."

I giggled. "Of course we do. We get along swimmingly."

An A+ Attitude

Good sportsmanship is a *must* in any sport! Do you have an A+ attitude or a bad case of sassitude? Take this quiz to find out.

① Do you give up easily or get frustrated if you can't master a skill right away?
   A+ Attitude Answer: Of course not! Practice makes perfect!

② Your backstroke is fab-u-lo-so but a teammate's having trouble. Will you offer to help?
   A+ Attitude Answer: Of course! Having a winning attitude means helping out when you can.

③ Do you exercise, eat healthy, and get enough rest?
   A+ Attitude Answer: Absolutely! An athlete knows that keeping fit is a full-time commitment to himself and to the team.

④ Do you complain when your coach calls an extra practice?
   A+ Attitude Answer: Never! The coach is in charge. Smile, give 110%, and set a good example for others.